Deck·the·Halls

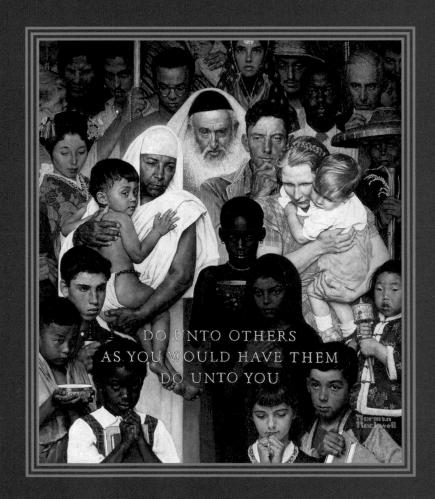

DO UNTO OTHERS
AS YOU WOULD HAVE THEM
DO UNTO YOU

NORMAN ROCKWELL

Deck the

Halls

Norman
Rockwell

ATHENEUM BOOKS FOR YOUNG READERS

New York   London   Toronto   Sydney

Norman Rockwell, my grandfather, painted more than four thousand images for magazine covers, calendars, advertisements, and story illustrations. He was born in 1894, published his first works in 1912, and continued to work until his death in 1978. His vast work needs to be looked at extensively to be properly appreciated, but, simply, a major appeal of his images is based on his showing an intimate, familiar, and humorous look at common events. Christmastime is a theme that Norman Rockwell visited frequently. In this book, the able editors at Atheneum have paired the words of "Deck the Halls" with Norman Rockwell images from Christmastime events.

The song "Deck the Halls" is simple, merry, and well-known. Most of us have sung it at a party or a family gathering while anticipating what Santa might bring us. The Norman Rockwell works in this collection also remind us of Christmastime moments: young ones looking in the chimney to see if Santa is coming; a few of the many faces of Santa; sledding and skating outings, favored holiday activities for those who live in such climates; and, of course, presents—coming and going.

I hope the readers enjoy this book and deck their own halls with good humor and merriment. I'm sure that is what my grandfather would have wanted.

—John Rockwell

Deck the halls

with boughs of holly,

Fa la la la la, la la la la.

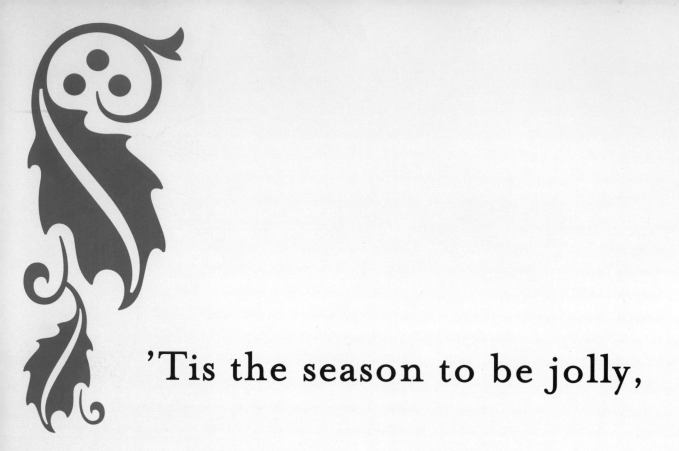

'Tis the season to be jolly,

Fa la la la la,

la la la la.

Don we now our gay apparel,

Fa la la

la la la,

la la la.

Troll the ancient Yule tide carol,

Fa la la la la,

la la la la.

See the blazing Yule before us,

Fa la la la la,

la la la la.

Strike the harp

and join the chorus,

Fa la la la la, la la la la.

Follow me in merry measure,

Fa la la

la la la,

la la la.

Norman Rockwell

While I tell of Yule tide treasure,

Fa la la la la,

la la la la.

Fast away the old year passes,

Fa la la la la,

la la la la.

Hail the new, ye lads and lasses,

Fa la la la la,

la la la la.

Sing we joyous, all together,

Fa la la

la la la,

la la la.

Heedless of the wind and weather,

Fa la la la la,

la la la la.

ILLUSTRATIONS CREDITS

p. 1
Golden Rule,
Saturday Evening Post cover,
April 1, 1961,
oil on canvas
(Photo courtesy of
Norman Rockwell Museum,
Stockbridge, Massachusetts).

p. 3
Christmas Packages,
American Boy cover,
December 1920,
oil on canvas
(Photo courtesy of
Norman Rockwell Museum,
Stockbridge, Massachusetts).

p. 7
*Oh Boy! It's Pop With a
New Plymouth!*,
Plymouth automobile
advertisement, 1951,
oil on canvas
(NRFA).

p. 9
Santa Claus,
Kellogg Company cereal
advertisement, 1950,
oil on canvas
(NRFA).

p. 11
Santa's Surprise,
Hallmark Christmas card, 1949,
watercolor on posterboard
(NRFA).

p. 13
Young Love Sledding,
Brown & Bigelow Four
Seasons calendar, 1949,
medium unknown
(NRFA).

p. 15
Is He Coming? (or *Little Boy
Looking up Chimney*),
Elks Magazine cover, December 1922,
oil on canvas
(© Christie's Images, Ltd., 1989).

p. 17
Christmas Trio,
Saturday Evening Post cover,
December 8, 1923,
oil on board
(The Norman Rockwell Art
Collection Trust,
Norman Rockwell Museum,
Stockbridge, Massachusetts).

p. 19
Jolly Postman,
Hallmark Christmas card, 1949,
watercolor on posterboard
(NRFA).

p. 21
They Remembered Me,
Leslie's cover,
December 22, 1917,
medium unknown
(BNRA).

p. 23
*Little Girl Looking Downstairs
at Christmas Party*,
McCall's cover,
December 1964,
medium unknown
(NRFA).

p. 25
The Story of Christmas,
Literary Digest cover,
December 24, 1921,
oil on canvas
(NRFA).

p. 27
*Merry Christmas, Grandma . . .
We Came in Our New Plymouth!*,
Plymouth automobile
advertisement, 1951,
medium unknown
(NRFA).

p. 29
Couple Ice Skating,
Red Cross Magazine cover,
March 1920,
oil on canvas
(Photo courtesy of
Norman Rockwell Museum,
Stockbridge, Massachusetts).

Atheneum Books for Young Readers
An imprint of Simon & Schuster Children's Publishing Division
1230 Avenue of the Americas, New York, New York 10020
Compilation of artwork copyright © 2008 by Norman Rockwell Family Agency
Book design by Krista Vossen
The text for this book is set in Mrs. Eaves and Wittenberger Fraktur.
Manufactured in China
First Edition
2 4 6 8 10 9 7 5 3 1
Library of Congress Cataloging-in-Publication Data
Rockwell, Norman, 1894–1978.
Deck the halls / [illustrations by] Norman Rockwell.—1st ed.
p.   cm.
Summary: Norman Rockwell images accompany this popular Christmas song.
ISBN-13: 978-1-4169-1771-7
ISBN-10: 1-4169-1771-3
1. Carols, English—Texts. 2. Christmas music—Texts. [1. Carols.
2. Christmas music.] I. Title.
PZ8.3.R598De 2008
782.42—dc22
[E]   2007037461